Lefty

LOUIE

BY CLAIRE ROLINCE

Lefty
Louie

BY CLAIRE ROLINCE

Illustrated by Claire Rolince
Computer Graphics by Drew Townsend

Louie is left-handed.
His sister is right-handed,
his mother is right-handed and
his father is right-handed.

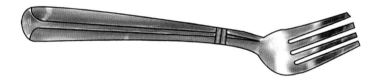

His parents noticed Louie
was left-handed the first
time he picked up his fork.

His sister noticed he was left-handed
the first time Louie threw a ball.

His teacher noticed he was
left-handed the first time
he picked up a pencil.

One day Louie's dad decided to take
Louie to play golf. Unfortunately the
pro shop didn't have any left-handed clubs.

So Louie had to play right-handed.
The next day Louie's dad took him
shopping for left-handed clubs.

Louie noticed that when he first
tried to use scissors, the paper
would not cut, it just bent.

He realized that if he wanted to
use scissors, he would have to
place them in his right hand.

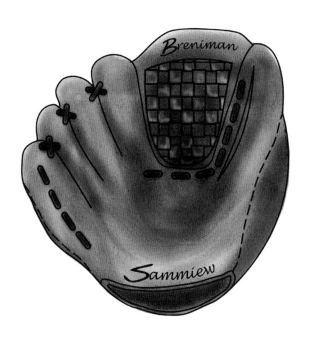

He learned that if he wanted to play baseball, he would have to buy a left-handed mitt. His father took him to two stores before they found one.

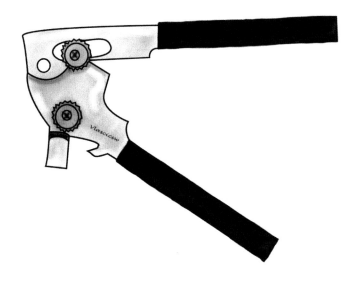

One day when Louie tried to open
a can of dog food for his puppy,
the can opener wouldn't work.

Again, Louie found that he
would have to use his right hand.

On his 10th birthday, Louie was given a great belt with baseball players on it. He loved that belt! But when he put it through the loops of his pants, the figures on the belt were upside down.

Louie realized that if he wanted
them right side up, he would have
to put his belt on the same way
as a right-handed person.

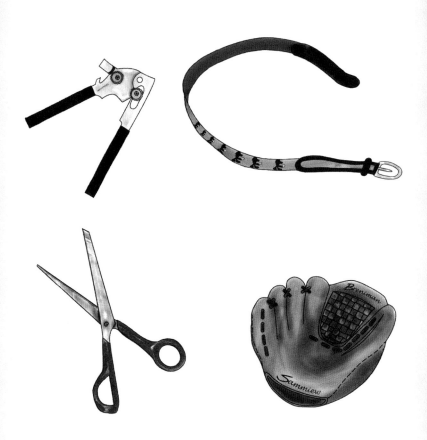

Louie was glad to be left-handed even though it meant he would need to do some things in the right-handed way.

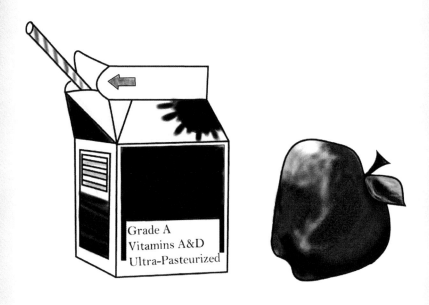

Louie enjoyed school, but his
favorite time of the day was lunch.
He was always hungry and eager
to eat with his friends.

If Louie sat between his friends,
he would bump elbows with them.
So he and his friends decided
it would be better if Louie
sat at the head of the table!

One day a new girl named Lucy
arrived in Louie's class. Lucy seemed
nice although she was very shy.

Lucy's desk was right in
front of Louie's desk. For the
first few days Lucy didn't take
part in any classroom activities.

But on the third day, when Lucy
raised her hand to answer a question,
Louie was thrilled! It wasn't because
Lucy wanted to answer a question;
it was because she raised her <u>left</u> hand!

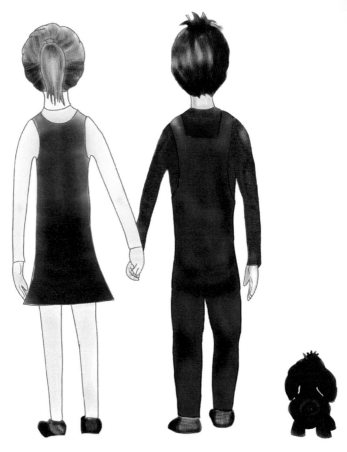

After school that day, Louie walked
Lucy home. They found they had
many things in common besides
being left-handed. Louie could tell
they would become best friends,
and for once he was right!